D0258386

ROCKHEAD

Rockhead the living mountain comes from the barren planet of Cojon, and battles Cosmo at G-Watch headquarters.

INTELLIGENCE	22
SPEED	65
STRENGTH	100
FREAK FACTOR	55
POWER OF THE UNIVERSE	60

HAMMERFIST

Hammerfist is an Ogron from Planet Ajax, with an iron punch that can knock out his opponents.

INTELLIGENCE	30
SPEED	31
STRENGTH	80
FREAK FACTOR	60
POWER OF THE UNIVERSE	52

MUCOSA

Mucosa, a slugoid from Planet Agar, has sliming glands all over his body, enabling him to trap enemies with his sticky slime.

INTELLIGENCE	54
SPEED	8
STRENGTH	15
FREAK FACTOR	95
POWER OF THE UNIVERSE	48

COSMO

Cosmo, an Earthling boy, possesses the Power of the Universe, and can use the Quantum Mutation Suit to transform into any alien form.

INTELLIGENCE	95
SPEED	60
STRENGTH	60
FREAK FACTOR	70
POWER OF THE UNIVERSE	100

www.alieninvaders.co.uk

www.alieninvaders.co.uk

www.alieninvaders.co.uk

www.alieninvaders.co.uk

ALIEN INVADERS

Don't miss any of the titles
in the ALIEN INVADERS series:

www.**kids**at**randomhouse**.co.uk

ALIEN INVADERS: ROCKHEAD, THE LIVING MOUNTAIN
A RED FOX BOOK 978 1 849 41230 8

First published in Great Britain by Red Fox,
an imprint of Random House Children's Books
A Random House Group Company

This edition published 2011

1 3 5 7 9 10 8 6 4 2

Text and illustrations copyright © David Sinden,
Guy Macdonald and Matthew Morgan, 2011
Cover illustrations, map and gaming cards by Dynamo Design
Interior illustrations by Siku
Designed by Nikalas Catlow

The right of David Sinden, Guy Macdonald and Matthew Morgan
to be identified as the author of this work has been asserted in accordance
with the Copyright, Designs and Patents Act 1988.

All rights reserved. No part of this publication may be reproduced, stored in
a retrieval system, or transmitted in any form or by any means, electronic,
mechanical, photocopying, recording or otherwise, without the prior
permission of the publishers.

The Random House Group Limited supports the Forest Stewardship
Council® (FSC®), the leading international forest certification organisation.
All our titles that are printed on Greenpeace approved FSC® certified
paper carry the FSC® logo. Our paper procurement policy can be found at
www.randomhouse.co.uk/environment

MIX
Paper from
responsible sources
FSC® C016897

Set in Century Schoolbook

Red Fox Books are published by
Random House Children's Books, 61–63 Uxbridge Road, London W5 5SA

www.**kids**at**randomhouse**.co.uk
www.**randomhouse**.co.uk

Addresses for companies within The Random House Group Limited can be
found at: www.randomhouse.co.uk/offices.htm

THE RANDOM HOUSE GROUP Limited Reg. No. 954009

A CIP catalogue record for this book is available from
the British Library.

Printed and bound in Great Britain by CPI Bookmarque,
Croydon, CR0 4TD

ALIEN INVADERS

MAX SILVER

ROCKHEAD
THE LIVING MOUNTAIN

RED FOX

THE GALAXY

PLANET ZAMAN

TARN BELT

DELTA QUADRANT

GAMMA QUADRANT

PLANET ABU

PLANET OCEANIA

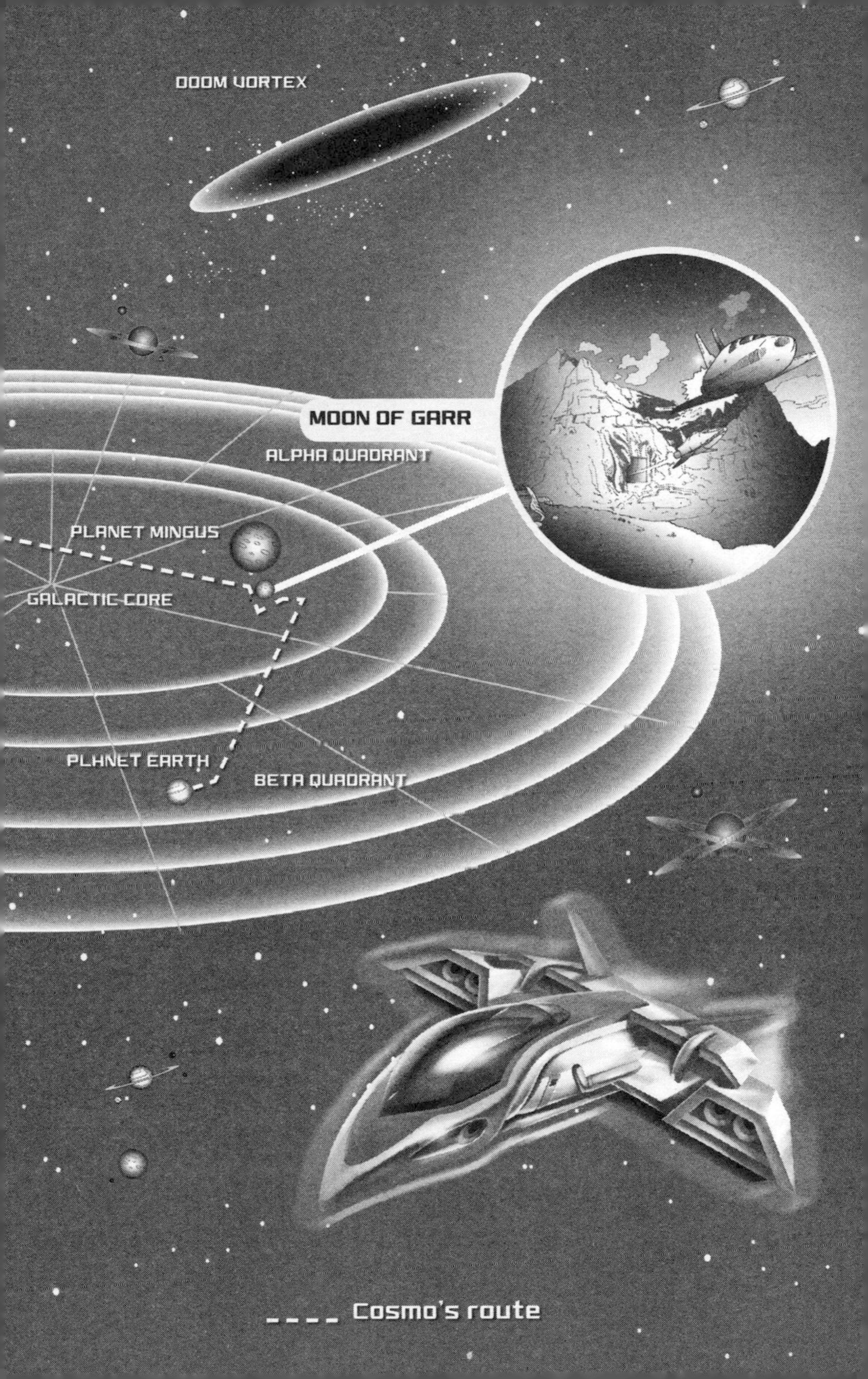

DOOM VORTEX

MOON OF GARR

ALPHA QUADRANT

PLANET MINGUS

GALACTIC CORE

PLHNET EARTH

BETA QUADRANT

_ _ _ _ Cosmo's route

ATTENTION, ALL EARTHLINGS!

MY NAME IS G1 AND I AM CHIEF OF THE GALAXY'S SECURITY FORCE, G-WATCH. I BRING YOU GRAVE NEWS.

IT IS THE YEAR 2121, AND OUR PLANETS ARE UNDER ATTACK FROM THE OUTLAW KAOS. HE IS BEAMING FIVE ALIEN INVADERS INTO THE GALAXY, COMMANDING THEM TO DESTROY IT. IF THEY SUCCEED, THIS WILL BE THE END OF US ALL.

A HERO MUST BE FOUND TO SAVE US: ONE WHO WILL VENTURE THROUGH THE TREACHEROUS REGIONS OF SPACE; ONE WITH AN UNCOMMON COURAGE WITH WHICH TO FIGHT THESE INVADERS; ONE WHO POSSESSES THE POWER OF THE UNIVERSE! THAT HERO IS AN EARTHLING BOY. HE IS OUR ONLY HOPE.

INVADER ALERT!

Deep in the galaxy, on a little-known crimson moon, G1, the Chief of Galactic Security, was working late. He wore a golden spacesuit and stood before a vast video wall inside G-Watch's secret headquarters, checking the satellite feeds. His silver eyes scanned the incoming images: hovercars whizzing through the Hwang metropolis, a space station orbiting the planet Juno, a convoy of freighters entering the Surian comet lanes. *No emergencies to attend to tonight*, he thought, relieved.

Suddenly the images flickered then froze as the satellite feeds jammed. G1's silver eyes widened with alarm as a new image of a hideous five-headed alien appeared on the video wall.

"Greetingsssss, G1," the alien hissed.

G1 folded his arms defiantly. "Kaos, you're spoiling my view."

The alien's five faces glowered at the Chief of Security. "This is your final chance, G1. Surrender the galaxy or I will unleash my forces."

The video image zoomed out, showing Kaos to be in the cargo hold of a large space battleship. Towering behind him were five monstrous aliens: one with a body of flames, another with fangs and spider-like legs, another with slimy writhing tentacles, one muscular and

glowing green, and one like a mountain of living rock.

G1 stared at the enormous aliens in shock.

Kaos's five faces grinned at him. "Meet Infernox, Zillah, Hydronix, Atomic and Rockhead. They're from the Doom Vortex, G1, and we've made a little deal together: I beam them into your lovely galaxy – and they destroy!"

"Kaos, I command you to stop!" G1 exclaimed.

But Kaos just laughed. "The galaxy will be mine, G1."

Rockhead, the enormous mountain-like alien, smashed his boulder-fists together. "*Destroy!*" he roared. Then the video wall flickered and the transmission ended.

The Chief of Security hurriedly unclipped a handheld communicator from his belt and spoke into it.

"G1 calling Agent Nuri."

A voice replied, "What is it, Chief?"

"The worst news imaginable," G1 said. "Kaos is sending in invaders from the Doom Vortex, commanding them to destroy our galaxy."

"From the Doom Vortex! But they'll be unstoppable, Chief!"

"We only have one hope. Fetch the Earthling at once."

"But Chief, he's still just a boy."

G1 looked up through a porthole into a starry sky. "We must hope he's ready. The future of the galaxy depends on him."

CHAPTER ONE

LEAVING PLANET EARTH

"The spaceship won't have left, will it, Mum?" Cosmo asked.

"We'd better hurry, Cosmo," his mum replied, rushing him in through the entrance of Heathrow Spaceport. They hurried across the concourse, pushing through crowds of people catching flights around the galaxy: families going on holiday to the paradise planet of Oceania, backpackers travelling to the

Wild Worlds, and businessmen attending
conferences on Megatroplia. There were
aliens coming in too, visiting Earth or
catching connecting flights to other
planets. Cosmo and his mum hurried
past a family of long-nosed Lavadians
carrying their luggage on their heads.
Cosmo dashed through the legs of a
Mollaxian as tall as the entrance hall,
and squeezed between bulbous Gloopons
eating burgers from the airport café.

He glanced at his reflection in the café's window and saw that his rucksack was half open, with a T-shirt hanging out – he'd packed in such a rush! He was wearing odd socks, one green and one red, and his wavy brown hair was unbrushed. *Oh, I wish I hadn't overslept,* he thought. He'd been so excited about the trip that he'd stayed up late asking Mum question after question about the galaxy.

It was the year 2121, and Cosmo
Santos, an eleven-year-old Earthling, was
off on his first trip to space. He'd won the
lucky ticket in *Space Explorers,* an
inter-planetary magazine. Thirty ticket-
winners from different planets were off
on a month-long tour of the galaxy!

Cosmo and his mum hurried into
the departures lounge and checked
the latest flight information on the
electronic board:

LUNAR EXPRESS – PROCEED TO BLAST BAY 6
OCEANIC ORBITAL – DELAYED DUE TO SOLAR STORMS
MARS SHUTTLE – PROCEED TO BLAST BAY 18
GALAXY TOUR – BOARDING BLAST BAY 20

"Galaxy Tour – that's me, Mum!"
Cosmo said excitedly.

They rushed through the crowd,
heading for a long travelator marked
BLAST BAYS 15–30.

"Excuse me . . . Sorry . . . Pardon me . . ."
Cosmo and his mum hopped onto the

travelator and it whisked them off like a conveyor belt, delivering them to BLAST BAY 20.

Cosmo saw a flight attendant at the bay's boarding gate. She had the cat-like eyes of an alien from Planet Kline.

"Ticket, please," she said.

Cosmo took a silver ticket from his jeans pocket and handed it to her. He waited excitedly as she ran her scanner finger over it.

"Welcome, Cosmo Santos, *Space Explorers'* winner from Earth," she said. "Looking forward to the tour, arc you?"

"You bet!" Cosmo replied.

"Then let's get you on board."

As the attendant opened the boarding gate, Cosmo glanced out of the blast bay's window, spotting a silver spaceship on the launch pad outside. *A Type-3 Cruiser – brilliant!* He'd flown one before on a computer game that his dad had given him called *Flight Simulator Pro*. Type-3s were fast! They had twin thrusters and hyperdrive capability. In the cockpit he could see its android pilot checking the controls.

Mum smoothed Cosmo's hair. "Goodbye then. I'll see you in a month," she said.

Cosmo looked up at her. "I'll miss you, Mum."

She smiled. "I wish your father could see you now."

"Me too," Cosmo said, and he gave her a hug.

"Mr Santos, if you'd like to follow me, we'd better be on our way," the flight attendant called from halfway across the boarding bridge.

Cosmo hurried after her to the cruiser's door and it slid open. He took a last look back at his mum, who was waving from the boarding gate. He waved too, then followed the attendant aboard.

Inside the cruiser, the other competition winners were already seated in travel pods, each of them an alien from another planet. Cosmo followed the flight attendant past them down the aisle, recognizing some of their species from *Alien Encyclopaedia*, an old e-book of his dad's. He noticed a Baluvian man with webbed hands sipping a can of Raiderade, a six-armed Krucian woman reading six copies of *Space Explorers*, and a Mervish man wearing four pairs of sunglasses to shade his eight eyes.

I wonder if I look as weird to them as they do to me, Cosmo thought.

The flight attendant stopped at an empty pod halfway down the cruiser. "This one is yours, Mr Santos."

"Thank you," Cosmo said, and he flopped down into the large cup-like seat. It had an entertainment console and a viewing sphere to see out of the side of the ship.

"You'll find a wordsworm in the arm compartment of your seat," the attendant told him. "The rest of the tour group might be a little difficult to understand without it!"

Cosmo glanced around at all the passengers, hearing them speaking to one another in alien languages. As the flight attendant moved away, he flipped open the arm compartment and saw a small orange worm wriggling in a dish.

A girl in the pod opposite spoke to him. "*Ning den. Voola pip-pip,*" she said. She wore a red spacesuit and had aqua-blue skin and pointy ears.

"Hang on a second – I can't understand you," Cosmo replied. He picked up the wordsworm and felt it wriggle in his fingers. Carefully he slid it into his ear and it burrowed down deep.

The girl spoke again and sounded completely different. "I said, 'It tickles at first but it's harmless,'" she repeated.

The wordsworm was translating her words as she spoke!

"We've got a pet one of these worms at school," Cosmo said. "And Mr Marshall, my Space Studies teacher, says it knows over twenty million galactic languages."

"You're native to Earth, I take it," the girl said.

"Yes," Cosmo replied. "This is my first trip to space. What planet are you from?"

"Etrusia in the Eagle Nebula. But I've been to many."

At that moment an announcement came over the passenger intercom. It was the android pilot speaking: *"Could all passengers please ensure that your luggage is stowed beneath your seats. We are preparing for blastoff."*

Cosmo stuffed his rucksack into a

compartment at the base of his pod. "Here we go," he said to the Etrusian girl opposite.

"I hope you're ready for an adventure," she replied.

"You bet."

The girl smiled, then looked away through her viewing sphere.

Cosmo glanced out from his, and saw the boarding bridge disconnect; then, over the intercom, the android pilot commenced countdown: *"Ten . . . nine . . . eight . . . seven . . ."*

Cosmo felt the launch pad rising and tilting, moving the cruiser through ninety degrees pointing up to the sky. He was now lying on his back in his seat. The engines began rumbling, louder and louder.

"Five . . . four . . . three . . ."

Cosmo felt his seat trembling.

"Two . . . one . . . blastoff!"

Suddenly the twin thrusters ignited, and fire filled the viewing sphere. With an almighty roar the space cruiser powered upwards into the air. The force was immense, causing the whole ship to rumble and pushing Cosmo back in his seat as it shot through the clouds. Cosmo had never travelled so fast before; in moments the cruiser had reached the edge of Earth's atmosphere, its fins glowing red-hot from the speed. All at once his viewing sphere darkened, and Cosmo saw the dotted lights of stars. He glanced back and saw Earth getting smaller behind him. It felt awesome. He was in space! *See you soon, Mum*, he thought, and he smiled as he sped off into the galaxy.

While Cosmo was looking out of the viewing sphere, unbeknown to him the blue-skinned Etrusian girl in the pod opposite unclipped a handheld

communicator from her belt. She pressed
its transmitter and whispered into it.

"This is Agent Nuri. The Earthling boy
is on his way."

"Time is pressing," a voice replied.
"Begin the Crash Test."

"But, sir—"

"No 'buts', Agent Nuri. The boy will
have the skills. The question is, will he
use them – does he *really* possess the
power?"

CHAPTER TWO

DANGER AT HYPERSPEED

As the cruiser flew through space, Cosmo felt himself floating off his seat in the zero gravity. He flicked a switch on his pod, activating its personal regravitator, and it pulled him back down. Drops of Raiderade from the Baluvian man's drink floated through the cabin, and he opened his mouth, catching one. It tasted like banana.

The cruiser passed the Moon; so close that Cosmo could make out the lights of lunar settlements. He saw other spaceships flying through the darkness: space freighters, Mars shuttles and delivery rockets. The cruiser's android pilot spoke over the intercom: "*Attention, all passengers. We are about to enter hyperdrive. Sit back and enjoy the flight.*"

Through the viewing sphere, Cosmo saw that they were approaching the beacons of a space hyperway, one of the high-speed routes through the galaxy. The cruiser accelerated and the stars turned to long white streaks. They were travelling at hyperspeed, blasting across star systems faster than the speed of light.

Cosmo settled into his pod and checked out its entertainment console, flicking through the 4D movie channel and alien cartoons. He played two games of *Stargon Superhero* and tried the tasty in-flight snacks: meteorbites and burgerbombs, washing them down with Raiderade.

This is the way to travel, Cosmo thought happily, and he leant back, looking out at the streaking starlight.

Cosmo took a tattered photograph from his pocket. It was of his dad in the cockpit of a Dragster 5000 spaceship. Cosmo's dad had worked in space for the galactic security force G-Watch and Cosmo longed to be a G-Watch agent one day, just like him. *I miss you, Dad*, he thought. More than two years ago Cosmo's dad had died in a space-crash, and Cosmo still thought about him every single day.

Suddenly the cruiser shuddered, and Cosmo glanced up from the photograph. He saw the Etrusian girl in the pod opposite, her blue skin looking pale with fright. "What was that shudder?" she asked.

"We probably just changed hyperlane," Cosmo replied. "We're travelling at over eight hundred million miles per hour."

But then the cruiser shuddered again, dipping and swerving violently.

Cosmo heard the android pilot over the intercom: *"Could all passengers stay ininininin . . . Error . . ."*

The android pilot sounded strange . . .

"Errooor . . . terminaaaate . . . shutdooooooooooooown."

Something's wrong! Cosmo thought.

The cruiser veered violently off the hyperway and came out of hyperspeed. He looked through the viewing sphere: they were heading straight for a huge planet made of shining liquid metal. Passengers started panicking, and an alien with stalked antenna eyes looked round from the pod in front, terrified.

The flight attendant's voice came over the intercom: *"Attention, all passengers. This is an emergency. Our android pilot has malfunctioned and we've lost control. Can anybody on board fly this spaceship?"*

Passengers screamed, fearing for their lives.

"If anyone can save this ship, please step forward now."

Cosmo looked around. No one was stepping forward. All the passengers were gripping their pods, screaming at the tops of their voices. *Someone has to do something or the cruiser's going to crash*, he thought. He remained calm, strangely calm; inside him a feeling was growing – whether it was courage or foolishness he couldn't tell, but it was like a force, making him want to stand up and volunteer, even though he knew it would be crazy. *I've flown a Type-3 Cruiser on Flight Simulator Pro*, he thought. *It's not real flying, but it's better than nothing.*

He switched off his pod's personal regravitator and floated upwards, pulling himself along the cabin's ceiling towards the cockpit.

"*I'll* do it!" he called. All the passengers were staring at him.

"The Earthling's going to save us!" cried a Sterovian man.

Cosmo's heart was thumping. He dared not tell them the truth: that he'd never flown a *real* spaceship before.

He pushed open the cockpit door and saw the flight attendant examining the android pilot, the control panel on its back open. She turned as Cosmo floated in. "I can't get it working!" she said.

Up ahead, through the cockpit's space-screen, Cosmo saw the liquid metal planet getting larger by the second. He glanced at the cruiser's controls and recognized them from *Flight Simulator Pro*!

I can *fly this ship*, he realized. "Check on the passengers," Cosmo told the flight attendant. "I think I can save us!"

CHAPTER
THREE

THE TEST

While the flight attendant stowed the
android pilot at the back of the cockpit
and went to check on the passengers,
Cosmo strapped himself in. *It's down
to me*, he thought as he took hold of the
steering column. He turned it hard to the
right, but felt the cruiser struggling to
realign. It was being drawn towards the
liquid metal planet.

"Planet Mingus is also known as the

ship-swallower," a little voice said. "It's magnetic."

Cosmo noticed a small bug-like robot staring up at him from the control desk.

It bleeped. "If we get any closer, it will suck us right in and we'll melt into it."

We need more thrust, Cosmo thought. He reached for the left thruster and fired it, swinging the cruiser free of Mingus's pull. "Er, thanks. Who are you?" he asked.

"I'm Brain-E, pilot's mate," the little robot replied.

"I'm Cosmo Santos."

"Well, Pilot Santos, I commend you on your bravery. Might I suggest you make an emergency landing on Garr? It's the moon that orbits Mingus."

Cosmo looked up through the space-screen and saw a tiny crimson moon above the metal planet. He aimed for it.

"As you enter Garr's atmosphere you'll need to be travelling at no more than four vectrons or we'll burn up," the robot said.

Cosmo glanced at the speedometer: *Eight vectrons!*

I need to slow us down – fast, he thought. He scanned the control desk looking for the switch that closed the fin vents.

The robot bleeped. "Where did you learn to fly?" it asked.

"Um . . . using a computer program my dad gave me. It has different spacecraft you can select." *Think, what closes the fin vents on a Type-3 cruiser? Ah, got it!* Cosmo flicked a switch on the side of the steering column and heard the hydraulic vents closing on the cruiser's fins. Garr was looming large in the spacescreen. *Seven vectrons . . .* The spaceship was slowing, but not enough. Cosmo felt the ship shudder violently as it met Garr's atmosphere. *Six vectrons . . .* He could barely keep hold of the steering column as

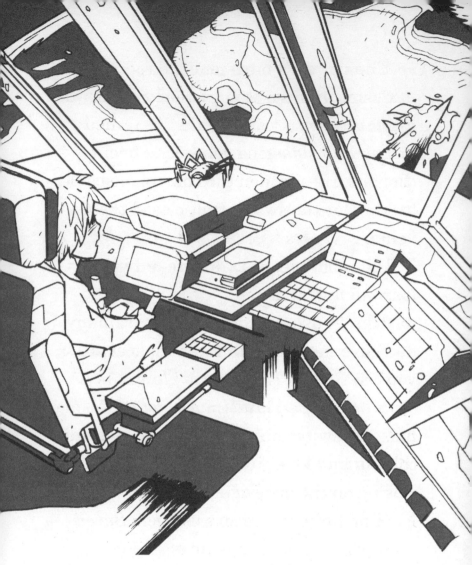

the cruiser shook and rattled under the pressure of the rapid entry ... *Five vectrons ... Still too fast,* Cosmo thought desperately. *We're going to break up!*

The cruiser's nose-cone glowed red-hot from atmospheric friction. Sweat was pouring down Cosmo's face. He pulled back on the steering column, reducing the entry angle, doing whatever he could to slow the cruiser down . . . *Four and a half vectrons . . . four and a quarter* . . . His arms were shaking; the ship's spacescreen was now glowing with the heat . . . *Four vectrons!*

The cruiser roared into Garr's crimson sky. He'd made it through! Far below he saw an alien landscape of scarlet mountains. Garr looked bare and desolate. He saw peaks lit by the glare of Planet Mingus, and canyons deep in shadow.

"Turn fifteen degrees west for the landing site," the little robot said.

As the cruiser descended, Cosmo turned the steering column. He checked the ship's height on the altimeter: *3,000 metres . . . 2,600 metres . . .*

Cosmo tilted the cruiser, flying down among the mountains and banking between two peaks. Below, he saw a long straight canyon to land in that was free of boulders and rocks. He smiled. *This is way better than* Flight Simulator Pro! he thought.

Cosmo felt for a lever at the base of the control desk. "Lowering the landing gear now," he said to the little robot. He pulled the lever and heard a deep clanging sound.

"Perfect," the little robot said. "Bring us in nice and steady."

As the cruiser descended into the canyon, Cosmo pulled the steering column back slightly, raising the nose-cone. He braced himself for landing – *three . . . two . . . one . . .* The spaceship's back wheels touched down with a bump; then its front wheels bounced a little and skidded, throwing up plumes of amber dust. Cosmo

turned two red handles, and the air
brakes roared. The wheels screeched and
the cruiser slowed to a standstill at the
very end of the canyon. Cosmo breathed a
huge sigh of relief. He'd done it – he'd just
landed a Type-3 cruiser on an alien moon!
All the passengers were safe!

"Well done, Master Cosmo," the little robot said. "Nice flying!"

Cosmo smiled. *We've made it!* He leaned back in his seat and looked through a porthole: he noticed the exit ramp being lowered from the side of the cruiser. The flight attendant and passengers were leaving the ship.

Brain-E bleeped. "Why don't you join them, Master Cosmo? It's perfectly safe to go outside. On Garr, gravity is nine over zero, the temperature is warm and the oxygen is plentiful."

Cosmo left the cockpit and peered out from the top of the cruiser's exit ramp. He felt hot air on his face and saw the metal planet Mingus in the sky. Then, as he walked down the ramp, the other passengers started clapping.

"Well done! The Earthling's a hero!" they cheered, then crowded round, shaking him by the hand.

Cosmo spoke to the flight attendant. "So what are we going to do now?" he asked her.

She smiled, and the crowd parted. Cosmo saw the blue-skinned Etrusian girl who'd been in the pod opposite coming towards him.

"What happens next depends on you, Cosmo Santos," she said.

"On *me*?" Cosmo asked. "What do you mean? And how do you know my name?" He was sure he hadn't told her.

"Sorry, but not everything here is as it seems," the girl said. "The emergency landing – it was a set-up, a test."

Cosmo looked at her, confused.

She pointed up at the space cruiser. "Take a look up there," she said.

Cosmo saw the android pilot back in its seat, waving from the cockpit.

"The pilot didn't really malfunction. It was a test to see if you *really* had it in you," she explained. "We wanted to know that you're ready. And you sure are!"

Cosmo stepped back, bewildered. "What's going on? Ready for what?" he asked.

The girl smiled again. "For G-Watch service," she told him. "The *Space Explorers* galaxy tour was a plan hatched by G-Watch to get you here in secret."

Cosmo looked around, seeing all the passengers smiling at him.

"My name is Agent Nuri," the girl said. "And everyone here works for G-Watch." She pointed across the canyon to the tallest of the mountains. "We've landed here on purpose. Over there is G-Watch's secret headquarters."

Cosmo squinted, seeing steps carved into the sheer rockface. Two enormous slabs of rock were sliding apart like doors. His mind was racing. "G-Watch? I'm really at G-Watch? This isn't a galaxy tour at all?"

"That's right," the Etrusian girl said. "G-Watch needs you. Come inside and I'll explain everything."

CHAPTER FOUR

G-WATCH NEEDS YOU

Cosmo followed Agent Nuri up the stone steps to the entrance in the mountain. He felt excited and puzzled all at once. He'd thought he was coming on a galaxy cruise, and now here he was, entering G-Watch headquarters. *What could G-Watch want with me?* he wondered.

At the top of the steps Nuri led Cosmo inside. In a cavernous room, he saw scientists working – testing vehicles and gadgets. The room was full of space buggies, hyperspeed engines, satellites, tanks, interstellar probes and even a solar-powered rocketship.

"Wow!" Cosmo said, trying to take it all in. "This place is so cool!"

"G-Watch headquarters have been based on Garr for hundreds of years, Cosmo," Agent Nuri said. "Top-secret work goes on here. It's the perfect hideaway; no spaceships come because it's so close to Planet Mingus."

Cosmo saw the G-Watch agents from the space cruiser coming in too, some rushing to workstations and others disappearing through dark doorways.

"But why am *I* here?" he asked.

Nuri smiled. "All will become clear if you follow me."

She led the way through the room and Cosmo looked around in wonder. He watched a mechanic testing the hydraulics of a gleaming silver space plough. It was huge.

"That's the new X1 Indestructible," Nuri explained. "It can power directly through asteroid storms."

They passed a scientist at a computer station setting the time on his watch. Cosmo saw it flashing blue, then it glowed, and the scientist whizzed into the air and vanished.

"Where did he go?" Cosmo asked Nuri.

"He's testing a prototype navicom," she replied. "It's an experimental technology we're trying to develop for transporting agents in emergencies." She glanced at the scientist's computer screen. "Oops, I don't think it's working properly yet. It looks like he's beamed himself into an asteroid belt!"

She led Cosmo across a section of floor marked with a grid. As he followed her, he found himself trekking through holographic landscapes: a steamy rainforest, then a freezing snowdrift, then a bone-dry desert. "What's this?"

"This is called the holodeck," Nuri said. "It's the latest in virtual reality – for training agents on how to survive in hostile environments." She stepped to a rack of hoverboards and took two down. She hopped onto one and slid the other over to Cosmo. "You do know how to hoverboard, I presume."

"Of course," Cosmo replied. His dad
had taught him and at school he was
captain of the hoverball team – a sport
played on hoverboards.

"Then follow me," she said. "It's the
best way to get around."

Cosmo stepped onto his hoverboard
and pressed his back foot down. The board
began zooming upwards like he was
surfing. He tilted left, veering round the
solar rocket, then followed Nuri up past a

storm satellite and through an opening in the stone ceiling to a level above. It was full of G-Watch spaceships: starfighters, microjets and stealth drones. *Wow!* Cosmo thought. Some had their thrusters burning as G-Watch scientists and mechanics tested them.

"The G-Watch spacefleet is always ready," Nuri told him. "These fly out on rescue missions in the event of galactic emergencies."

Cosmo noticed a mechanic examining the engine of a white spaceship with laser cannons set into its nose. "Hey, is that a Dragster 5000?" he asked, surfing closer to take a look. "My dad flew one of these! He was a G-Watch agent. Did you know him, Nuri?"

"Not personally," Nuri replied. "But I have heard of him – James Santos, I believe."

"Yes, that's him."

"Well, this is a more recent model than he would have flown – the Dragster 7000. It's the most advanced G-Watch spacecraft to date."

Cosmo ran his hand along its gleaming hull. *This is my kind of spaceship*, he thought. *It's amazing!*

"Follow me," Nuri said briskly. "There's something that I need you to see a few levels up."

Cosmo followed her up through the levels of G-Watch headquarters, through a room containing a platoon of armed G-Watch battle-droids, then a surveillance room with a video wall and agents working at control desks.

Nuri stopped inside a white room with a tinted-glass cabinet and two large objects hidden under plastic sheets. "This is what I wanted to show you," she said. "It's top-secret."

Pulling off the first sheet, Nuri

revealed a deep-space reconnaissance
probe squashed to a slab of metal. It had
a clawed footprint as big as a man
pressed into it. Then Nuri removed the
second sheet, revealing half of a twisted
G-Watch satellite. Buried in it was a
razor-sharp fang as long as Cosmo's arm.
Cosmo stared in shock.

"These were recovered from far beyond our galaxy, in the Doom Vortex, Cosmo. Both have been savagely attacked."

Yikes! Cosmo thought. "By what, Nuri?"

"By aliens of unimaginable evil."

Cosmo gulped, feeling shaken by what Nuri was saying.

"You won't have learned about these aliens in Space Studies at your school. These fearsome creatures have evolved in the most hostile outer regions of the universe. It's only in recent years that they've been discovered."

Cosmo stared at the clawed print and the fang, trying to imagine the fearsome aliens they'd come from. "But why are you showing these to me?" he asked, puzzled.

"Because five such creatures are coming to destroy our galaxy, Cosmo. They take orders from an outlaw called Kaos, and we need *you* to stop them."

CHAPTER FIVE

THE POWER

Cosmo stared in shock at the crushed reconnaissance probe and the large fang buried in the satellite. "You seriously want *me* to fight enormous aliens? Are you crazy?!" he asked Agent Nuri.

"Not crazy at all," she replied. "G1 will explain."

The air shimmered and, as if by magic, a man in a golden spacesuit appeared. "Thank you, Agent Nuri," he said.

Cosmo blinked, startled. "Where did you come from?"

The man looked down at Cosmo with kind silver eyes. "Welcome, Cosmo. My name is G1, Chief of G-Watch, and I have much to tell you should you choose to accept your mission."

"But why me?" Cosmo asked.

"Because of who you are and what's inside you," G1 replied, eyeing Cosmo seriously. "Inside you, we believe there to be a unique power. What made you step up to save the space cruiser from crashing?"

Cosmo remembered the urge he felt before he volunteered to save the cruiser. "I only did what I thought was right," he replied.

"We believe you were drawing on something special inside of you, Cosmo – a power that's present in all life forms, but in you to an exceptional degree.

It can manifest itself as courage, honour, truth and even intense physical energy."

"I was just being me," Cosmo said, stunned. "I don't have any superpowers."

G1 smiled warmly. "Not a superpower like in stories, but a real power. It's the power of the universe, Cosmo."

Cosmo stepped back, stunned.

"Other people have noticed it too," G1 continued. "I knew your father, Cosmo. He was our greatest agent, and he alerted us to something special in you. We have been keeping watch over you from space for several years now, monitoring your progress with interest."

"Monitoring me? Why?"

"Should you one day choose to join us here. Your father has already trained you in rudimentary agent skills, Cosmo. Did you not realize?"

"Trained me?"

G1's silver eyes twinkled. 'You can fly any spaceship. *Flight Simulator Pro* is no computer game; it is a G-Watch training program. You can hoverboard, ski, scuba dive, and most of all you think like an agent, instinctively knowing the right thing to do."

Cosmo thought of his father, remembering all the brilliant things they'd done together. *So Dad was teaching me to be a G-Watch agent all along!* he thought, amazed. But he still felt apprehensive.

"Surely I can't fight these huge invaders," Cosmo said. "Can I?"

"You have the power, Cosmo," G1 said simply. "It is stronger in you than in any other. You are our only hope."

* * *

Meanwhile, deep in the Doom Vortex, battleship *Oblivion* was anchored behind a dead star. Kaos paced inside its cockpit, his five heads locked in debate.

"We must strike where it hurts," one head said to his others.

"We must destroy their fuel supplies and hijack their trade routes," another head added.

"We'll spread disease, fear and panic."

"The galaxy will beg for mercy!"

"G-Watch must suffer first. Without them to protect the galaxy, every star, planet and moon will be ours for the taking. Send in Rockhead, the living mountain!"

His five heads all cheered at once. "Send in Rockhead!"

A scrawny purple rat squeaked from the cockpit floor and Kaos's heads peered down at it. "Don't just stand there, Wugrat. Fetch the navicom."

The rat scurried to a metal shelf and took down a small crystal disk, holding it in its mouth. It scampered after Kaos down a long corridor.

The alien was chuckling to himself. "The secrets to the navicom transporter unit are ours," one head said.

"G-Watch is no match for us," another smirked.

Kaos opened the door to the cargo hold. Inside, five fearsome aliens were waiting.

"So, you wish to leave the Doom Vortex, eh?" Kaos said to them. "You know the deal. I beam you into the galaxy, and you fight for me."

"Yes, master!" the aliens roared.

"Rockhead, you're up first. Destination: Garr."

The huge rock alien smashed his boulder-like fists together. "G-Watch is over!" he bellowed.

"Wugrat, give that thing to me," Kaos said, reaching down to the rat and snatching the navicom transporter disk from its mouth. "Have you set it for Garr?"

The wugrat squeaked again and Kaos twisted the crystal's outer edge like a dial. He reached up and fastened it to Rockhead's arm. The navicom began flashing.

"Go get them," Kaos said to the invader.

Rockhead stomped to the centre of the cargo hold. *"Destroy!"*

The roof of the cargo hold opened, and Rockhead looked up at the swirling stars of the vortex. A blue light began to glow from the navicom and with a *whoosh* Rockhead shot out of the battleship and vanished into space.

CHAPTER SIX

QUANTUM MUTATION SUIT

Back at G-Watch headquarters, Cosmo's mind boggled from everything that the G-Watch chief was telling him.

G1 stepped to the tinted-glass cabinet. "I have something to show you, Cosmo." He opened it and took out a spacesuit. "This spacesuit is G-Watch's most advanced piece of technology. It's called the Quantum Mutation Suit and has been designed especially for you. It's a body armour for extreme combat." G1 handed it to Cosmo. "Try it on."

Body armour? Cosmo touched it. It didn't feel like body armour – it was flexible, like cloth. He held it up. It looked too big for him. "Er, I'm not sure this will fit me . . ."

G1 smiled. "We hadn't intended you to join us until you were a grown man."

"It should adjust," Nuri said encouragingly. "Try it on." She fetched him spaceboots, gloves and a helmet from the cabinet too.

Cosmo gingerly stepped into the spacesuit. He slipped his arms in, feeling small and foolish. Its sleeves hung down over his hands. He awkwardly pulled on the gloves, boots and helmet. All of a sudden the Quantum Mutation Suit began rippling. Cosmo could feel it moving over his skin as if it was alive.

"It's working, Chief!" Nuri said to G1.

G1 smiled. "You have nothing to fear, Cosmo."

Cosmo felt the suit tightening to fit him, moulding itself like a second skin. It started to glow electric blue.

"It's reacting to the power inside you, Cosmo," G1 said. "It's activating."

As G1 spoke, the helmet's visor lit up like a transparent computer screen in front of Cosmo's eyes. Words appeared: SYSTEMS CHECK STARTING. Lines of computer code raced across it.

"What's it doing now?" Cosmo asked.

"This helmet acts as a control module," Nuri said. She peered in at him through the visor. "It's just warming up. Some strange things should happen now, but you're perfectly safe."

The suit sparked as if lightning was running through it. Cosmo could feel it fusing with him, and his arms and legs tingled, hot one moment and cold the next. Suddenly his body started to change. Cosmo saw green reptilian scales appear on his torso, then on his arms, then on his legs. They were spreading over him – he was growing an alien skin!

He felt a little freaked out, but it didn't hurt – he just looked different. Then he felt the scales softening and gasped, seeing fine hairs sprouting through them. His skin was changing again into fur, thick black fur like a bear's. He took a deep breath and tried to stay calm.

"What's it doing to me?"

"Don't be alarmed, Cosmo," G1 reassured him. "It's just running through a few mutations."

Mutations? This is so weird! Cosmo thought. His body was changing before his very eyes. His furry skin transformed to prickly spines then to red feathers. *Feathers! How's this possible?* he wondered. Next his body turned sticky like slime, then red-hot like molten lava, then icy. It was incredible!

His hands and feet tingled – the gloves and boots were fusing too. They glowed brightly, changing shape. Cosmo now had long hooked talons where his feet should have been. His hands turned into large pincers and he snapped them together like a crab. He tried it again and they changed into paws. The next moment, his arms turned into long suckered tentacles. *Like a sea monster's!* Cosmo thought. He shook the tentacles and they changed into large leathery wings. *An alien dragon!* He beat the wings like he was flying.

On the visor, he saw more words appear: SYSTEMS CHECK COMPLETE. His wings receded, becoming arms again, and Cosmo returned to normal, dressed in the Quantum Mutation Suit. "How did it do all that?" he asked, dumbfounded.

"The Quantum Mutation Suit is made

from a fabric infused with particles from
the beginning of time when the universe
first came into existence," G1 explained.
"The same particles from which all life
came. Only you can activate it though,
with the power that you have inside you –
the power of the universe!"

"You can transform into any alien life

form you choose," Nuri said. "Just say 'SCAN' into the helmet's sensor to select your body type. It's voice-controlled."

"SCAN," Cosmo said, and on the visor's digital display, pictures of aliens appeared one after the other: winged aliens, underwater aliens, storm aliens . . . with details of their species, origins and features. The mutation suit was scrolling through its databank.

"It's 'MUTATE' to transform, and if you wish to return to normal just say 'RESET'. The sensors will still be embedded in your new form."

"I can really become any of these

aliens?" Cosmo asked. "This is amazing!" He lifted the visor on the helmet and looked at Nuri and G1 in astonishment.

"It's G-Watch's most formidable invention, a suit that will give you infinite capabilities," G1 told him. "Should you choose to accept your mission."

"The galaxy needs you, Cosmo," Nuri said. "Are you ready to fight?"

Suddenly Cosmo realized the seriousness of the situation. "And I'm the only person who can do this?"

"That's right," G1 said gravely.

Cosmo paused a moment. *There'll be extreme danger. I might not survive . . .*

But inside him he felt an urge to say yes. "I'll do it!" he exclaimed.

G1 and Nuri both smiled.

"Splendid," G1 said, and he unclipped a handheld communicator from his belt. He spoke into it: "Surveillance, we're ready to go—" He paused as a voice replied. "Where's it heading?" G1 asked, his face clouded with concern. "Alert all agents! Mobilize the battle-droids! This is a RED ALERT."

G1 switched off his communicator, then turned to Cosmo and Nuri. "It appears that Kaos has navicom technology," he said. "Our interplanetary scanners have detected the first of the invaders beaming through the galaxy, and it's heading for our headquarters here on Garr." He approached the wall and touched his hand to a round sensor. The wall slid open and crimson daylight flooded into the secret headquarters.

Cosmo looked out over the mountains and heard a sound like thunder. He saw something enormous hurtling through the sky at phenomenal speed. It looked like a meteor. It came down between the mountains and struck the base of the canyon with a massive *boom*, sending up dust and rocks.

As the dust cleared, Cosmo gazed down and saw something emerging from a huge crater. It was a monstrous alien with a body of solid rock. It was ten times the size of an Earthling man and had fists like boulders. It stomped towards G-Watch headquarters, swinging a punch at the space cruiser on the landing strip. The cruiser spun end over end and crunched against the mountainside.

The monstrous alien looked up the mountain and roared, "I am Rockhead, and I have come to *destroy you!*"

CHAPTER SEVEN

MUTATE AND FIGHT!

"It's massive!" Cosmo said nervously. "How can I possibly fight that thing?"

Cosmo watched in horror as Rockhead lifted the crumpled space cruiser above his head. The massive rock alien hurled it at G-Watch headquarters, smashing it against the entrance. The mountain shook with the force of the blow.

"He's going to knock this place down, G1!" Nuri said.

Cosmo saw G-Watch battle-droids marching out from the main entrance, laser guns at the ready. There were a hundred of them – the entire platoon. They took up positions on the steps, ten rows of soldiers one behind the other, all pointing their lasers at Rockhead.

"In the name of the free galaxy, halt!" the droid commander shouted.

But instead Rockhead charged.

The battle-droids opened fire, shooting

at the invader, but their laser beams bounced off him. Rockhead thundered up the steps. He stamped on the first line of droids, squashing them like tin cans.

G1 spoke into his communicator: "All agents to battle stations!" He turned to

Cosmo. "It's time to fight," he said. "If you feel you are ready, meet us in the main hall." Then he vanished into thin air.

There was a loud *boom*. Cosmo looked down the mountainside and saw Rockhead charging at the huge stone doors. He'd swept aside the droid soldiers and was trying to force his way in. *He mustn't make it*, Cosmo thought.

"Come on Cosmo – downstairs!" Nuri called, zooming off on her hoverboard.

But Cosmo felt an energy welling inside him. *It's the power of the universe*, he thought. It was giving him courage.

"I'll see you at the bottom," he replied. He hopped onto his hoverboard and whizzed out of the opening in the top of the mountain. Cosmo made the board dip down, aiming it at Rockhead, then flicked down the visor on his helmet.

"SCAN," he said into the voice sensor. On the visor's digital display, images

of alien creatures appeared as the
Quantum Mutation Suit scrolled through
its databank: a two-headed vorpwolf, a
laser-eyed xarg, a fiery lavabear, a high-
voltage electrax . . . Cosmo compared
alien heights, weights and features.
Which alien can beat a living mountain?
he wondered. Then he spotted a huge,
muscular alien with a massive metal fist.

ALIEN: HAMMERFIST
SPECIES: OGRON
ORIGIN: PLANET AJAX
HEIGHT: 10.4 METRES
WEIGHT: 2.2 TONNES
FEATURE: IRON PUNCH

"MUTATE," Cosmo said into the
helmet's sensor. He felt his whole body
tingle; then he started to grow wider and
taller. His skeleton was re-forming itself,
his bones lengthening and thickening. It
was incredible! He was growing to over
ten metres tall, his skin stretching as

muscles bulged out all over his body. One
of his fists was enormous and made of
solid metal. He was Hammerfist!

The hoverboard sank under his massive
weight and he leaped down, landing by the
entrance with a thud. Around him, battle-
droids lay broken and twisted, but as
Hammerfist, Cosmo felt strong. He strode
past the mangled space cruiser towards

Rockhead, clenching his huge metal fist. "Hey, you. It's no entry!" he called.

Rockhead turned to face him. "No one can stop me!" the invader roared back, and he smashed his boulder-fists down, shaking the ground like an earthquake. He charged into Cosmo, driving him hard against the rockface. Cosmo felt his breath being knocked out of him. The invader's force was immense. "Prepare to be crushed!" Rockhead shouted.

Cosmo tried to push the rock alien off, but there was no way to budge him, even using Hammerfist's huge muscles. It was like wrestling with a living mountain!

Rockhead swung his boulder-fist, but Cosmo ducked just in time, and it smashed into the mountainside, sending rocks flying.

"You call that a fist?" Cosmo roared. "*This* is a fist!" He wrenched his metal fist free and slammed it hard against

Rockhead, sending sparks flying. The huge creature staggered backwards, stumbling over fallen battle-droids.

Cosmo threw another punch: this time his metal fist struck Rockhead's stomach. The alien doubled up under the force of the impact.

"You don't look so tough now, Rockhead. Is Hammerfist too powerful for you?"

As Hammerfist, Cosmo felt invincible. He swung his arm round in a circle, his metal fist gathering speed like a demolition ball. He landed a powerful uppercut to Rockhead's chin, and the alien's jaw cracked. "Give up, Rockhead, or Hammerfist will bust you!" Cosmo yelled.

But the blows only made Rockhead angrier. "Never!" he roared. He reached round, picked up the space cruiser by its cockpit and swung it at Cosmo. It

smashed into him, sending him tumbling down the steps, head over heels. He landed in a heap at the bottom.

"Hammerfist cannot stop me!" Rockhead bellowed.

Cosmo lay on the ground, battered and bruised from the fight. He could feel his energy waning, the power leaving him: Hammerfist's molecular pattern was breaking up. The Quantum Mutation Suit was failing. "RESET," he said, and Hammerfist's muscles began receding. Cosmo was shrinking, turning back into a boy.

Rockhead stared down at him from the top of the steps and laughed. "Ha! Ha! Haaaaaaaaaah! Look at yourself now. You are no match for me!"

Behind the alien, Cosmo saw the doors sliding apart. Six G-Watch battle-tanks trundled out from the mountain. They opened fire on Rockhead, blasting him with their sonic cannons.

The invader roared as the blasts hit, his craggy body shaking with the force of each impact. "That makes me mad!" he yelled.

Rockhead stomped to the lead tank and grabbed hold of its cannon. He lifted the tank off the ground and hurled it aside like a toy, then raised his fists, smashing them down on two more.

The huge doors slid closed again as the remaining tanks continued pummelling Rockhead with their sonic cannonfire.

"I shall let myself in another way," the fearsome alien roared. Rockhead stomped over the tanks and began to scale the sheer mountainside. He punched at the rock as he climbed – he was trying to force his way into G-Watch headquarters through the mountain itself!

CHAPTER EIGHT

"I WILL CRUSH YOU!"

Cosmo looked up in horror, seeing
Rockhead trying to smash his way into
G-Watch. Then he saw Nuri clambering
from the top of a mangled tank onto the
broken droids.

"Are you OK?" he called to her.

"We have to stop him, Cosmo!" Nuri
replied.

I need to climb up after him, Cosmo
thought, watching the invader on the

mountainside. "SCAN," he said into the helmet's voice sensor.

The Quantum Mutation Suit searched its databank, and once again, images of alien creatures scrolled down in front of Cosmo's eyes: a storm-eating torrnatron, a thousand-eyed telescopterix, an ice-breathing freezoth, a fanged wolverax . . . *What could climb?* He saw an image of a six-armed ape-like alien.

ALIEN: GRAPLAX
SPECIES: BURATANG
ORIGIN: PLANET ZOTH
HEIGHT: 7.6 METRES
WEIGHT: 1.2 TONNES
FEATURE: SIX LONG CLIMBING ARMS

Perfect, Cosmo thought. "MUTATE!"

He felt his body tingling as it changed, growing bigger and bigger, his skin turning to fur. He could feel his sides splitting and arms extending, six of them, each over five metres long, with ape-like hands. He beat his six fists against his chest. "Not so fast, Rockhead!" he called.

As Graplax, Cosmo ran like an ape, bounding along on his knuckles, taking the steps ten at a time. He vaulted over the broken droids and the wrecked tanks, then leaped up onto the sheer rockface.

"Go, Cosmo!" Nuri shouted. Cosmo looked down and saw her give him a thumbs-up then dash back into headquarters.

Cosmo gripped the mountainside with his six strong hands and began pulling himself up towards Rockhead, arm over arm.

The invader was already high up the mountain, smashing his fists against the rock, trying to find a weak spot where he could punch his way through. G-Watch headquarters was shaking. Boulders were dropping off the rockface like an avalanche, and cracks were beginning to appear in the mountainside.

All of a sudden the invader managed to punch his fist right through the rock, pushing his arm inside. Cosmo heard the screech of twisting metal and saw Rockhead pull out a bank of G-Watch control desks, throwing them down the mountainside. He saw agents tumbling down too, shooting grappling hooks from their utility belts to snag hold of the rockface and stop themselves falling.

"Hey, leave them alone!" Cosmo yelled.

Rockhead threw a bank of computers at him, trying to knock him off. But Cosmo swung across the face of the mountain, avoiding the debris. He grabbed hold of a rocky overhang.

"I will crush you!" Rockhead roared.

Cosmo pulled himself higher, clambering up in pursuit of the invader. Faster and faster he climbed, his six

arms working together. With one arm outstretched, he reached for the ledge beside Rockhead; then, with his other five hands, he tried to pull the enormous alien off the mountain.

"Graplax is taking you down, Rockhead!"

Cosmo wrenched one of his opponent's legs away from the rockface, then grabbed the other. Rockhead lost his footing, but had his arm pushed through the hole he'd punched in the mountain, stopping himself falling.

Cosmo and Rockhead were now locked together. Cosmo was pulling as hard as he could, but Rockhead was holding fast.

Just then, a section of the mountainside slid open, and Cosmo heard the roar of engines. Spaceships from the G-Watch battle-fleet flew out: starfighters, microjets and stealth drones.

While Cosmo wrestled with the alien,

trying to pull him off the mountainside, the spaceships circled Rockhead, blasting him with laser fire.

Rockhead swiped at a starfighter, swatting it and sending it spinning out of control. Its pilot managed to eject just in time, and the craft hit the ground, exploding on impact. Cosmo saw that the pilot was Nuri. She opened her parachute and floated down past him. "You can do it, Cosmo!" she called out to him.

But even as Graplax, Cosmo couldn't prise Rockhead off the mountain.

Rockhead shouted, "You won't stop me!" and once again smashed his fist into the rock. Cracks spread out and, suddenly, a chunk of the mountainside caved in.

Rockhead and Graplax both fell through the hole into the G-Watch surveillance room. Down they went, crashing through the levels, one after the

other, landing with a thud on the floor of the main cavern.

Cosmo felt shaken and battered, his power waning. "RESET," he said weakly. He felt his body tingling and he started shrinking, mutating back into a boy.

CHAPTER NINE

THE SWORD

Cosmo scrambled out of the way as
Rockhead rose to his feet. They were
inside G-Watch headquarters, standing
among the vehicles in the main cavern.
Laser guns were firing: G-Watch agents
were taking up positions and shooting at
the invader.

Rockhead laughed at Cosmo. "G-Watch
is finished! The galaxy is entering a new
age, the Age of Kaos!" He smashed his

fist down on the X1 Indestructible space plough, breaking it in two, then hurled a space buggy at the wall. G-Watch agents dived for cover as the fearsome alien pushed over the solar-powered rocket, sending it crashing to the floor.

"Hey, cut that out!" Cosmo yelled.

Rockhead turned and snarled, "Not given up yet, puny Earthling?"

The invader strode closer, his rocky

fists raised, ready to pulverize Cosmo.

One more try, Cosmo thought desperately. "SCAN," he said into his helmet's sensor. The Quantum Mutation Suit scanned through alien life forms, their images appearing on the visor's digital display. *How can I defeat Rockhead?* he wondered. An image of a jelly-like slime alien flashed across the visor, giving him an idea.

ALIEN: MUCOSA
SPECIES: SLUGOID
ORIGIN: PLANET AGAR
HEIGHT: 3.2 METRES
WEIGHT: 8 TONNES
FEATURE: SLIMING GLANDS

"MUTATE."

Cosmo felt himself changing once again, his body growing huge, squidgy and shapeless. It felt as if his skeleton had suddenly gone soft. Stalk eyes protruded from his huge jelly-like body, and slime started oozing from every pore.

As Mucosa, Cosmo faced Rockhead in the centre of the cavern.

The invader let out a roar of revulsion at the sight of his opponent. "Prepare to be squished, Slimeball!"

Cosmo held his ground, his stalk eyes spotting the rock alien clench his boulder-fists, ready to attack. Rockhead punched Cosmo with all his might . . . but Cosmo's wobbly body absorbed the power like jelly and he held his ground. The invader's fist sprang back, covered in slime.

Cosmo gurgled, "You can't hurt me, Rockhead."

The invader swung again, even harder. But again Cosmo absorbed the power of the blow, his blob-like body rippling. Rockhead punched with his other fist, but it was still no use. The invader's strength was useless against Mucosa. And with every punch Rockhead was getting covered in slime: thick, gooey slime that was slowing him down, making him heavy and sticky.

Cosmo oozed slime even more, leaking mucus from glands all over his body and even spewing goo from his mouth. He was attacking the invader with gallons of slugoid slime! Rockhead tried to throw a punch, but he slipped and slid, struggling to stay on his feet.

"I knew you'd come to a sticky end, Rockhead," Cosmo gurgled.

His mighty opponent roared with rage and swung his fist again, but lost his balance and toppled over. He tried to get up, but couldn't get a grip on the slippery floor. "You slimeball!" he shouted in fury.

Mucosa had done his work and the invader was down, but the slugoid had no way of dispatching him.

"RESET," Cosmo said, and his jelly-like body tingled as he turned back into a boy wearing the Quantum Mutation Suit. He looked at the G-Watch agents taking cover behind upturned and damaged vehicles. "Rockhead, you don't belong here," Cosmo said firmly.

Looking at the destruction around him, Cosmo felt his power surging, stronger than before, more physical this time, like electricity flowing through his veins. He could feel an invincible courage spreading through him, and the mutation suit glowed, sparking brightly. Suddenly, white and blue light burst from Cosmo's hand like lightning. He stared at it, shocked.

"It's your power, Cosmo," Nuri called. "Use it!"

The lightning-like energy was taking the form of a sword. Cosmo raised it and charged at Rockhead. "The power of the universe is in me!" he cried.

The alien roared as the power sword struck, "NO!" Then a look of hatred spread over his craggy features.

Cosmo could feel his power running through the sword into the invader. He felt defiant and strong, every molecule of his body vibrating, his power locked in battle with Rockhead's hatred. All at once cracks began spreading over the rock alien's body. Then, in an explosion of light, the invader vanished.

CHAPTER TEN

FOUR MORE TO COME

Cosmo stepped out of the pool of slime and heard the sound of applause. He looked round and saw Nuri and all the G-Watch agents clapping and cheering.

"Cosmo, you did it!" Nuri called.

G1 put his hand on Cosmo's shoulder. "You saved us, Cosmo. You've saved G-Watch," he said.

Cosmo wiped slime off his gloved hand. "The sword ... where did that come from?" he asked.

"From inside you, Cosmo. It's a physical extension of your power – strong enough to destroy evil."

Cosmo took off his glove, but he couldn't see any trace of the sword now.

G1 smiled. "It will come again, Cosmo, when you next need it. Now that you have seen your power in action, you must decide whether to use it further and continue your mission. There are four more alien invaders set to attack: four more battles to fight. Are you willing to face them?"

Cosmo thought for a moment. *Four more invaders – this was going to be dangerous!* Back on Earth his mum would still be thinking he was on a galactic cruise.

But the galaxy needed him . . .

"I'll do it!" he said.

All the G-Watch agents in the cavern

cheered. "Way to go, Cosmo!"

G1 smiled, then picked up two hoverboards and handed one to Cosmo. "Follow me, I have a surprise for you," he told him.

They surfed up a level to the G-Watch spacefleet bay. Maintenance bots were already repairing the huge hole in the floor where Rockhead and Graplax had crashed through. The bay's takeoff hatch was open to the sky and mechanics were busy servicing the G-Watch battle-fleet after its fight with Rockhead. Amidst the dust and activity, Cosmo saw a group of G-Watch scientists standing proudly beside the Dragster 7000 spaceship – the ship was hovering off the ground, its thrusters throbbing.

"It's fuelled up and ready to go," one of them said.

G1 looked at Cosmo. "Hop in then. It's yours."

"My own spaceship!"

"Our finest," G1 said.

The ship lowered, and a door in its side slid open. Cosmo stepped in. It was brilliant: gleaming new and equipped with the latest technology. On the control desk a small bug-like robot bleeped. "Welcome aboard, Master Cosmo," it said.

It was Brain-E, the little robot that had helped him land the cruiser. "G-Watch brainbot reporting for duty!" it said.

"Brain-E, are you coming as well?"

"If I may, Master Cosmo."

"Me too," said a voice behind Cosmo. He glanced round and saw Agent Nuri coming aboard. "If you'd like a co-pilot, that is," she grinned.

Cosmo laughed. "You bet. This is going to be a blast!"

He placed his helmet on the control desk and sat in the pilot's seat. Through the spacescreen he looked out at the crimson Garr sky. He could just make out Planet Mingus dipping behind the mountains.

He noticed G1 speaking into a handheld communicator, then a moment later the silver-eyed chief approached the Dragster's door. "Well, you'd better buckle up and set off," he said.

"Already, Chief?" Nuri asked.

"Our interplanetary scanners have just picked up a second invader beaming through the galaxy's Dyad-24 star system. We believe it to be the fire alien, Infernox. He is heading in the direction of the jungle planet Zaman, where many of the galaxy's medicines originate. It would appear that Kaos is targeting vital galactic resources."

"OK, G1, we're on to it," Cosmo said. He switched on the Dragster's thrusters. "Nuri, could you set the route to Zaman, please?"

"Yes, Captain."

Cosmo pressed a button, closing the ship's door, then released the docking clamps. He pulled the throttle and, with a blast, the Dragster 7000 shot out from G-Watch's secret headquarters, speeding him away on his mission.

"Infernox, we're coming to get you!"

Join Cosmo on his next **ALIEN INVADERS** mission. He must face – and defeat

INFERNOX
THE FIRESTARTER

INVADER ALERT!

In the wild jungle of Planet Zaman, robot DEL-8 rolled between the trees on its caterpillar tracks, its forklift arms carrying a crate of sparkling berries. It trundled into a large clearing where Planet Zaman's only building stood – the Eco-Tec Medicines Laboratory. The delivery-bot swivelled its camera eye, blinking in the lilac sunlight, then rolled in through the laboratory door.

"Starberries for sorting," it announced through its voicebox.

Inside, hundreds more robots were at work, creating advanced galactic medicines from the plants that grew in the jungles of Zaman. Robot DEL-8 tipped the crate of starberries out onto a conveyor belt, where a team of sorting-bots began removing the berries' stalks with their pincers and cleaning them with electric brushes.

DEL-8 selected a tray of the juiciest berries and took them over to the processing area, where processor-bots were waiting, piston arms raised.

"Juicy starberries for pulping," DEL-8 said, placing the tray on a metal workbench.

The processor-bots squashed the berries to a pulp, then extractor-bots rolled in and sucked up the paste with their hoses, sending it through into their mixing tanks. There was a whirr as they separated the chemicals, then squirted a sticky syrup into jars. The team of robots were preparing starberry syrup, one of the most precious medicines in the galaxy. It was the only cure for comet cough, a terrible illness carried in the toxic vapour trails of comets. Packager-bots packed the jars of syrup into boxes, ready to be collected by cargo ships and distributed to the galaxy's planets.

All through the laboratory, teams of robots were busy turning jungle plants into medicines: glimpan-tree wax for sun blisters, zinger-pollen spray for gravity sickness, mistlemoss cream for dongaloids, oozing-buckthorn ointment for tentacle tension, and even nut-nectar bug-eye drops.

Robot DEL-8 rolled out of the door to fetch another crate. But as it headed into the jungle, a loud roar sounded overhead. Its camera eye swivelled, glancing up through the trees. Its circuits whirred, puzzled by what it saw: a huge ball of fire was hurtling down through the sky. DEL-8's processor calculated that the fireball was heading straight for the laboratory. It bleeped in alarm: "Danger! Danger!"

Suddenly the huge ball of fire smashed down onto the building. In a massive explosion, robots, machinery and medicines were blasted in all directions. DEL-8 was sent flying backwards, smashing into a tree trunk.

"Emergency!" it called, crashing to the ground. It tried to right itself, but its caterpillar tracks had jammed. Its camera eye focused on the burning laboratory. "Emergency!"

Flames raged through the building and thick black smoke rose high into the sky. Then, out of the flames stepped an enormous alien creature.

DEL-8 bleeped fearfully, seeing the alien grinning. "Intruder! Intruder!"

The alien glowed red-hot and towered even higher than the burning laboratory. He roared menacingly, spewing fire from his mouth like a volcano.

"I am Infernox, and by order of Kaos I've come to set this planet ablaze!"

CHAPTER ONE
THE MISSION

"Destination: Planet Zaman!" Cosmo said, blasting the Dragster 7000 spaceship away from Garr. "Point me in the right direction, Nuri."

"Programming route co-ordinates now," his co-pilot, Agent Nuri, replied. She was tapping numbers into the spaceship's navigation console, a look of concentration on her blue-skinned face. "Done," she said. She tapped the spacescreen, activating its star plotter, and words lit up on the glass:

DESTINATION: PLANET ZAMAN

STAR SYSTEM: DYAD-24

ROUTE: HYPERWAY 55 FROM THE BIG DIPPER CONSTELLATION

DISTANCE: 2.6 BILLION MILES

Cosmo felt excited. Through the spacescreen, in the distance, he could see a pattern of seven stars shaped like a frying pan – the Big Dipper constellation. "Are you ready for another adventure, Nuri?"

"I sure am, Cosmo!"

"Then it's full speed ahead!" Cosmo nudged the steering column, turning towards the Big Dipper, and increased speed to eleven vectrons. They were on their way.

Cosmo Santos was an eleven-year-old Earthling boy on a mission for the galactic security force G-Watch to save the galaxy from five alien invaders. The invaders were being beamed in by the galactic outlaw Kaos, using navicom transportation devices, and were under orders to destroy the galaxy. So far, Cosmo had defeated the first of them – Rockhead, the living mountain – in a fierce battle on Garr. Now he was heading west to the jungle planet, Zaman, to face the second invader, the fire alien Infernox.

Cosmo dipped the Dragster's fins, shooting through the stars of the Big Dipper. Up ahead, the flashing lights of space beacons marked the entry to Hyperway 55, one of the galaxy's high-speed space lanes. Cosmo wove the Dragster between them then opened a panel on its steering column, revealing a silver switch.

"Engaging hyperdrive, Nuri," he said.

Cosmo flicked the switch and was thrust back into his seat by the force of the acceleration. The stars in the spacescreen turned to bright white streaks as the Dragster 7000 shot across the galaxy at hyperspeed, twice the speed of light.

"Are you ready to face the enemy, Cosmo?" Nuri asked.

"I think so," Cosmo replied, a little apprehensively.

"You can do it! Trust in your power, Cosmo," Nuri told him.

Well, there's no turning back now, Cosmo thought. As he blasted along the hyperway, a feeling of courage began to well up inside him, and his spacesuit glowed. He was wearing G-Watch's most advanced piece of technology – the Quantum Mutation Suit, a living body armour infused with particles from the beginning of the universe. Activated by the power inside him, it enabled Cosmo to mutate into alien forms to fight any opponent.

"We're nearly there," Nuri said. "Exit hyperway in seven seconds."

"Already?" Cosmo asked. "That was two-point-six billion miles? Wow, hyperspeed is fast!"

"... *four ... three ... two ... one ...*"

Cosmo flicked the hyperdrive switch back and turned the steering column. His ears popped as the spaceship veered off the hyperway then slowed to seven vectrons. Through the spacescreen he saw two enormous stars orbited by a cluster of vibrantly coloured planets.

"Welcome to the Dyad-24 star system," Nuri said. She tapped the screen, activating its star plotter, and words lit up on the glass beside each astral object.

PLANET UMAX ... PLANET OBON ... PLANET JUNOK ... PLANET ZAMAN! Cosmo read, seeing a large green planet straight ahead. He powered the Dragster towards it, slowing to two vectrons as they entered the planet's atmosphere. He switched the spaceship to planetary mode, and the cabin pressure self-adjusted as the ship flew into a lilac sky. Cosmo looked down and saw a vast jungle of trees veined with silver rivers. It was incredible – far bigger than any jungle on Earth. From his vantage point in the Dragster he could see the trees covering hills and valleys as far as the horizon.

"Zaman's jungle contains some of the

most incredible plants in the universe," Nuri said. "It's where many of the galaxy's medicines originate from."

Cosmo took the Dragster low over the treetops to take a closer look. Some of the trees were enormous, and he saw alien creatures too: a herd of horned beasts grazing in a clearing; a flock of four-winged parrots flying alongside the Dragster. It was truly wild! He zigzagged along a winding river, then burst through the spray from a colossal waterfall.

Nuri checked the navigation console. "G-Watch's scanners plotted the invader's trajectory, and calculated that it would have struck around here. Keep an eye out."

Cosmo peered down apprehensively. *Where are you, Infernox?* he thought.

Nuri reached across the control desk and gently tapped a bug-like robot. "Brain-E, wake up – we've arrived."

Brain-E, the ship's brainbot, bleeped and its lights came on. "Good day, Miss Nuri."

"I've never known a robot sleep as much as you do, Brain-E," Nuri laughed. "Tell us what you know about the alien invader Infernox."

The little robot stretched its six metal legs, then bleeped again, searching its databank. "According to my data, Infernox is an alien of volcanic origin from an ever-expanding sun in the Doom Vortex."

Cosmo gulped. He knew from his encounter with the first alien, Rockhead, how powerful aliens from the distant Doom Vortex could be.

"Infernox is a firestarter," the brainbot continued. "And can emit immense heat in the form of fireballs."

"Fireballs in a medicine jungle! That doesn't sound good," Cosmo said. He peered over the treetops and saw a column of smoke rising into the sky. "I think I've spotted where he struck. There's a fire over there!"

He looked down. Below, a building in a clearing was ablaze. Cosmo flew closer, looking anxiously to see if Infernox was still around, but thick black smoke was pouring into the sky and fierce flames raged thirty metres high. "I can't see properly. There's too much smoke," he said.

Nuri gasped. "The fire's out of control."

"We have to put it out before it spreads to the jungle," Cosmo told her.

Nuri went to check the kit shelves at the back of the cockpit. "We've only got a handheld flame-freezer, Cosmo," she said, grabbing a gun-like gadget. "It's designed for putting out engine fires, not huge fires like that. Those flames are too big!"

Cosmo banked the Dragster and circled above the burning building, desperately wondering what to do. The flames leaped around the spacescreen, the spaceship's engines making the air swirl violently.

"Careful, Cosmo," Nuri said. "You're pulling the flames towards us!"

That gave Cosmo an idea. *A crazy idea. But it might just work*, he thought. He pulled back the throttle, increasing the Dragster's speed. "Hold on tight, Nuri!"

"Cosmo, why are you accelerating?" she asked, alarmed.

"I'm going to make a whirlwind, and try to suck these flames into the air," Cosmo replied, his heart racing. "I'm going to use the Dragster to put out the fire!"

Find out what happens in INFERNOX – THE FIRESTARTER . . .